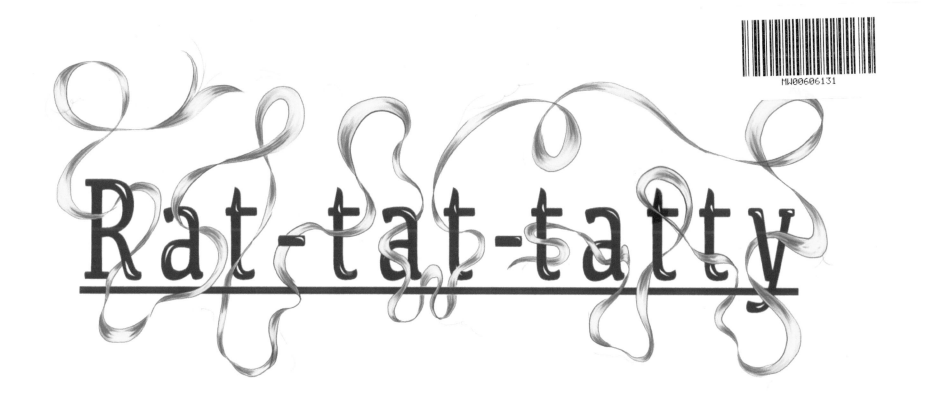

Rat-tat-tatty

Deseret Nelson

Illustrated by Deseret Nelson and Sevena Izatt

ISBN 978-1-63630-842-5 (Paperback)
ISBN 978-1-63630-843-2 (Hardcover)
ISBN 978-1-63630-844-9 (Digital)

Covenant Books, Inc.
11661 Hwy 707
Murrells Inlet, SC 29576
www.covenantbooks.com

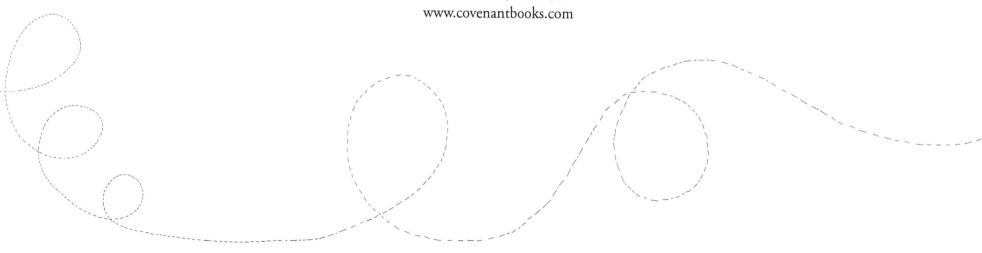

Although my kids have given me lots of inspiration,
this book is dedicated to my husband
Richie who has given me so much support
and the courage to make this a reality.

I love you, Squeeze!

—Deseret

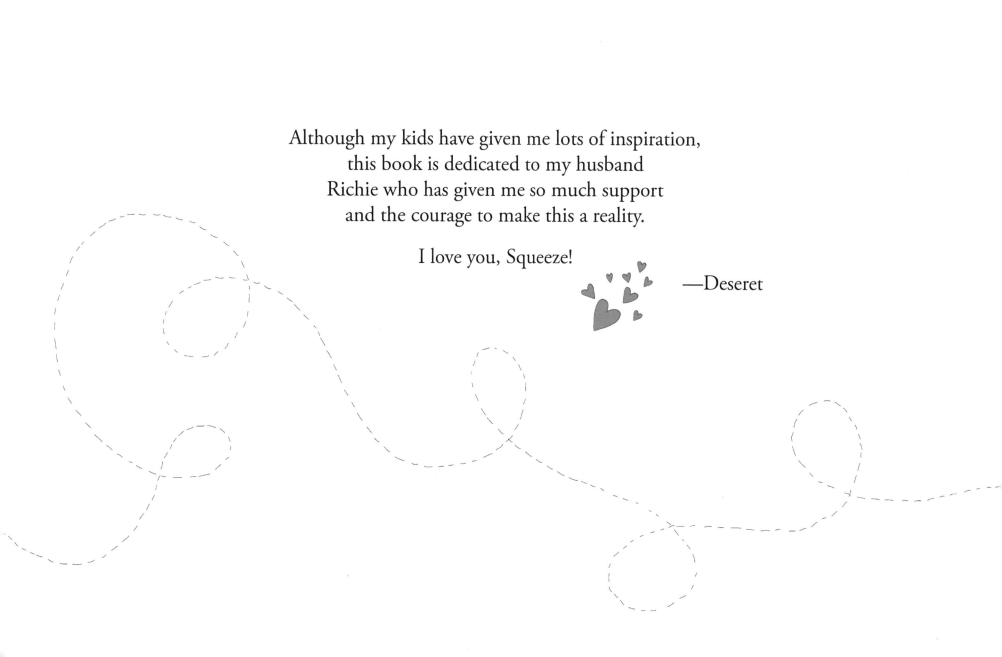

The hair on your head is so proper and neat. Not a hair out of place so shiny and sleek.

Bows and ribbons tie it up just right. Not a Rat-tat-tatty you'll see in sight.

"A Rat–tat–tatty," you might say, "what's that?"

Well...

Rat–tat–tatties make the knots in your hair. And how they get there? This I will share:

When your hair is loose as you sleep at night, Rat-tat-tatties think it quite all right,

to come on in and begin to dance. All dressed up in pajama pants.

5

They begin with a wiggle, and
then do a little jiggle.

Then they start to giggle as they roll all around.

7

They'll even throw your hair like confetti on the ground.

When the Rat-tat-tatties are done dancing all night, they make a nest and say, "Sleep tight."

And then by morning when you look in the mirror, you might just say, "What has happened here!"

10

Don't be surprised if they start to bite, cuz when you *whip* out your brush, they'll hang on tight.

This is the part where it might get nasty. You may have to yell,

Get out

There could be a small struggle or even a BIG fight.

You may have
to pull with all of
your might.

15

Here's a small tip: Don't pull from the top.

Start at the bottom and work your way up.

Those Rat-tat-tatties will soon lose their grip, and if you keep pulling, they'll start to slip.

16

But here's a small warning for you, if I may:
Be sure to brush your hair every day, cuz those Rat-tat-tatties will indeed want to stay.

Yes, they'll stay, and more will come, and all that dancing will never be done.

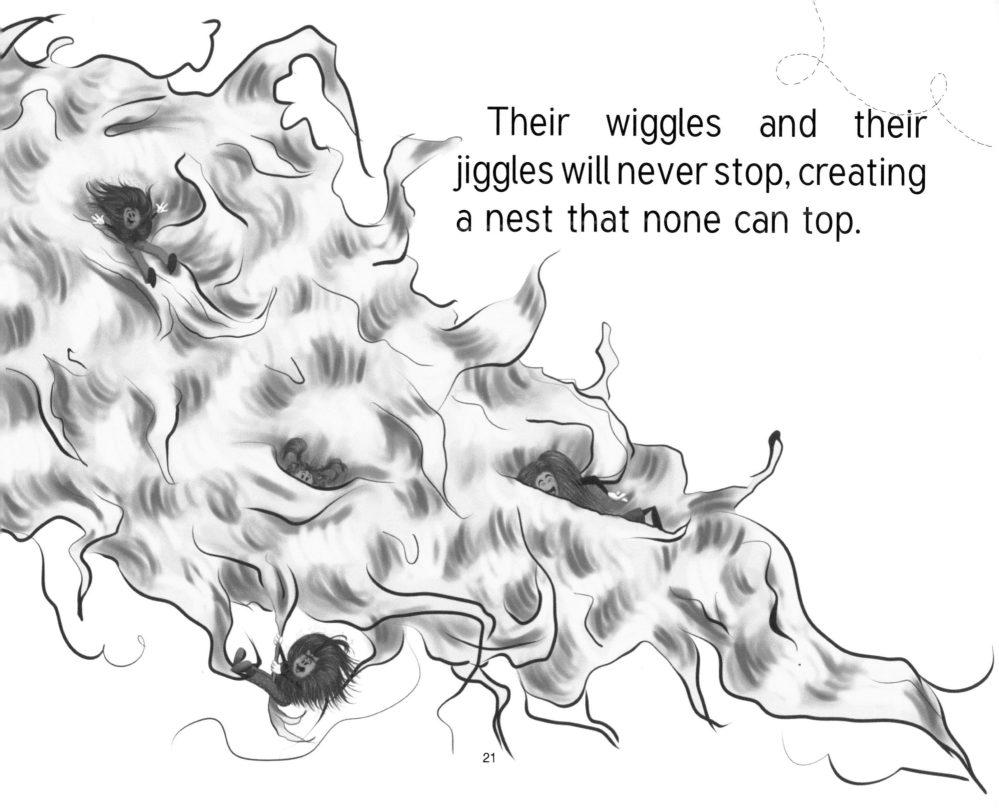

Their wiggles and their jiggles will never stop, creating a nest that none can top.

By then the only way to get them to leave is to call a barber and say, "Shave me please."

So to keep those Rat-tat-tatties at bay, pull your hair back in the most proper way.

23

Keeping your hair cut short, that works too. But it's okay if you like the Rat–tat–tatty zoo. With their wiggles and their jiggles and all their dancing about, if you like that look, who am I to doubt?

24

No one should judge you. Just go on with your day. Rockin' that nest the Rat-tat-tatty way.

The End

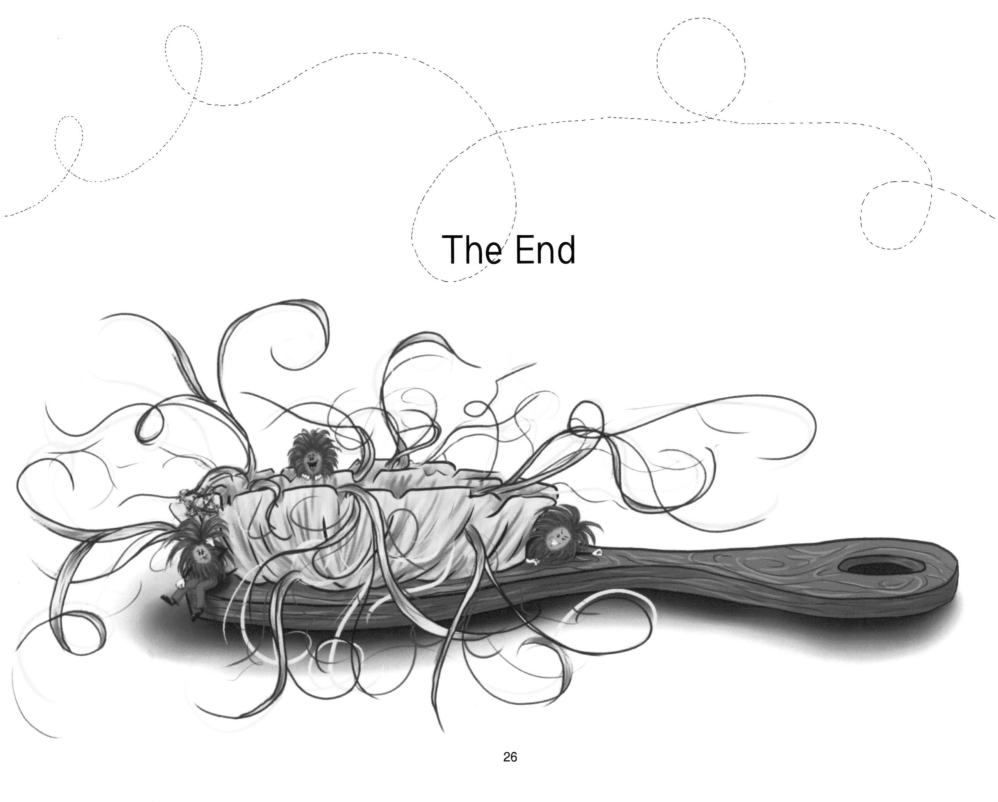

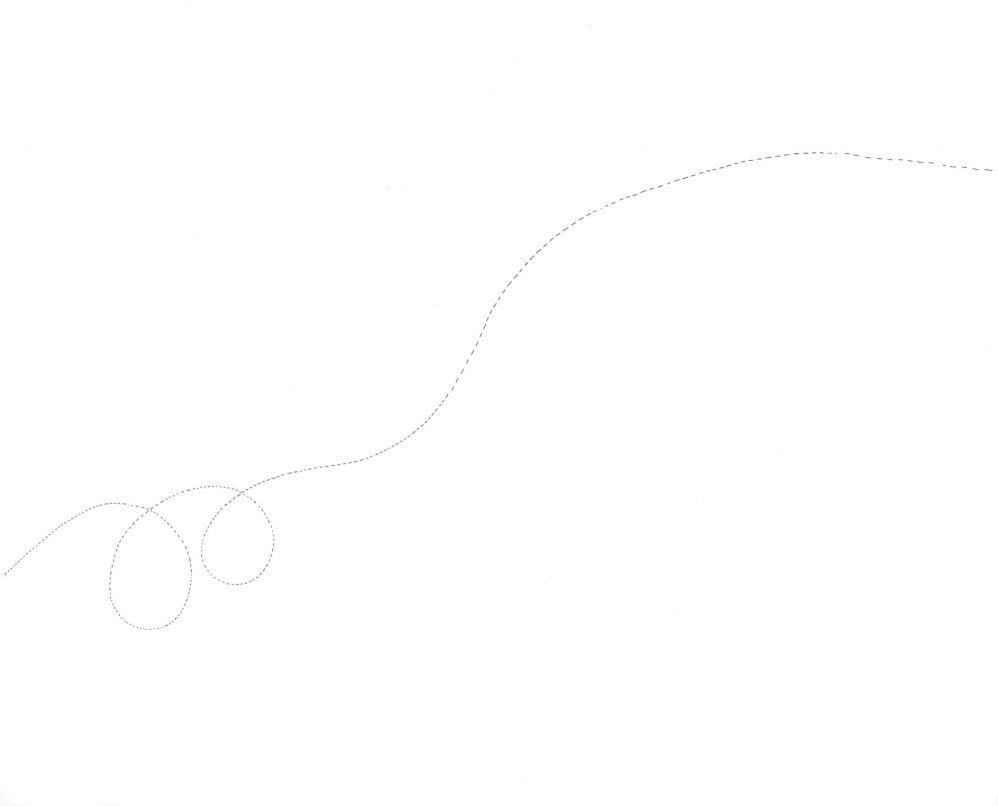

ABOUT THE AUTHOR

Deseret Nelson enjoys the outdoors, watching movies, and most of all the time spent with family and good friends. Homeschooling her four wonderful kids brings no shortage of inspiration and laughter to things she writes. They, alongside her husband, Richard, live in Oregon.

CPSIA information can be obtained
at www.ICGtesting.com
Printed in the USA
BVHW090030231121
622229BV00003B/80